Magic Animal Café

Published by Sweet Cherry Publishing Limited
Unit 36, Vulcan House,
Vulcan Road,
Leicester, LE5 3EF
United Kingdom

First published in the UK in 2022
2022 edition

2 4 6 8 10 9 7 5 3 1

ISBN: 978-1-78226-932-8

© Stella Tarakson

Magic Animal Café: Robbie the Rebel Squirrel

Cover design by Fabiana Attanasio and Jessica Walters
Illustrations by Fabiana Attanasio

www.sweetcherrypublishing.com

Printed and bound in Turkey

Magic Animal Café
Robbie the Rebel Squirrel

Stella Tarakson

Illustrated by
Fabiana Attanasio

Chapter One

Ellie stared at the torn piece of newspaper in her hands and gasped.

'What's wrong?' Blake asked, stopping what he was doing.

'This photo ... it's my great-grandfather.'

'He was in the paper? How come?'

Ellie and Blake had been tearing off the papers that had covered up the old building's windows. The papers

had been there for many years. Now that the building was ready to become a new cat café, it was time to let in some light and show it off to the world.

When Ellie didn't answer, Blake looked over her shoulder. He read the headline out loud: '"Local vet committed to" – something. Hey, it's ripped! Where's the rest of it?'

'I don't know.' Ellie stared at the photo of a man with messy hair, an untidy beard and intense eyes. 'He used to own this building. He left it to Mum when he died a few years ago. I've never met him, but Mum once showed me photos of him. He looked

different, but ... he was a vet, just like this says. It *must* be him.'

'Is he the one who had a few –' Blake tapped the side of his head '– problems?'

'Yeah.' Ellie stared at the photo in the newspaper. Her great-grandfather hadn't looked so messy in the photos Mum had shown her. In those, he had slicked-back hair and a neatly trimmed beard. His eyes had shone with happiness. Ellie wondered what had happened to change him.

'So, what's the story with him?'
Blake asked

Ellie shrugged. 'Mum never said.'

'You can ask her now.'

'I could, but Mum doesn't like talking about him. She was pretty upset when he died.'

After a moment, Blake asked: 'What does "committed" mean?'

'I'm not sure what it means here,' Ellie admitted, looking at the paper again. 'This says, "committed to" ... and the rest is gone.'

'It was his phone, wasn't it?' Blake asked. 'The magic one?'

When Ellie first moved into the building, she'd found a mysterious old trunk locked away in a cupboard. Inside the trunk was an old-fashioned black telephone. After dialling a number written on it, Ellie and Blake were both stunned and delighted to discover that they were able to talk to animals. For the first time, Ellie wondered whether her great-grandfather was able to do that too. Maybe he was the one who wrote the numbers on the dial!

Suddenly, Ellie was seized with a need to find out more about her great-grandfather.

'Where's the rest of the article? Let's check the floor.'

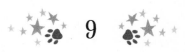

Ellie and Blake fell to their knees and started searching through the pile of torn pages. Blake's Labrador puppy joined in enthusiastically, digging with his oversized paws.

'No, Choccy!' Blake scolded. 'Your claws are ripping up the papers!'

'I help,' the puppy panted, his

tongue hanging out with the effort.

'Don't help. Just leave it alone. I said stop!' Blake grabbed his dog's collar and held it with both hands. 'Ellie, you keep looking.'

'I'm trying, but there's nothing here.'

'There must be. Unless Choccy ate it ...'

'Is something wrong, kids?' Ellie's mum came in from the storage room. Her long flowing dress swept the floor behind her.

'I dropped something,' Ellie said, not looking her mum in the eye. 'Blake's helping me look for it.'

'Right, well I'll leave you to it,' her mum said. 'I've got to get something from upstairs.' Bracelets jangling,

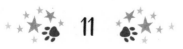

Ellie's mum headed off through the back of the café towards the flats' rear entrance.

'Why don't you ask her about your great-grandad?' Blake suggested.

Ellie shook her head. 'I don't want to upset her. Let's see what we can find out ourselves first.'

'I help Ellie!' Choccy lunged back into the pile and started scrabbling among the papers again.

'I'll put him in the backyard,' Blake said, gripping his wriggling puppy. 'You keep looking.'

Ellie nodded as Blake dragged his energetic pet outside. She took a deep breath. All was silent for a few minutes as she scanned page after page of old news stories. Rather than rummaging around aimlessly, she placed everything into neat piles. If they weren't about her great-grandad, she put them aside.

The papers all dated from long ago, most likely when her great-grandfather had first moved out. The building had lain empty for years until her mum took over and turned it into their home and café.

Ellie was so absorbed in her task that she didn't hear the tapping

on the window. It grew louder and louder, and more and more frenzied. Startled, Ellie looked up.

A large white bird was pecking on the glass and glaring at her. It was Shazza, an Australian Cockatoo who'd accidentally found herself living in Britain. She was bold and demanding, and rather hot tempered.

'Ellie, come quickly!' the bird squawked. 'I need your help. There's an emergency!'

Chapter Two

'An emergency?' Ellie called through the window, jumping to her feet. 'What do you mean?'

Ellie and Blake had met the bird earlier that day. Shazza now lived in a big oak tree in the park across the road. The children had become friends with her ... in a way. Shazza was loud and very bossy. The destructive

cockatoo was quite a handful!

But Shazza was also homesick and sad. Her greatest wish was to go home to Australia, but the kids didn't know how to send her back. Once the cockatoo discovered that Blake was also Australian, and – more importantly – that he also ate Vegemite sandwiches, she wanted to live with him.

Blake wasn't allowed another pet, so Shazza had to stay in the park. But there was a problem. Unless they could find a way to stop it, the park was going to be redeveloped. A massive leisure centre was going to be built on it, all concrete and steel and glass. There'd be no grass, no trees, and nowhere for the park's animals to live.

'Come and see!' Shazza replied. 'Come right now and fix my emergency!'

Ellie didn't know what to make of it. Shazza tended to exaggerate, but Ellie couldn't take the chance of ignoring the bird if something was really wrong.

'Coming!' Ellie crammed the piece of newspaper into her jeans pocket. She headed out the café's front door, hoping that her mum wouldn't come back and toss out all the newspaper scraps that still littered the floor.

 17

'What's the matter?' Ellie asked
Shazza, who'd waddled to the
doorway to meet her.

'It's terrible. It's awful! Come
quickly. Aiirrk!' The big bird hauled
herself up into the air. With a flap
of her powerful wings, she shot
across the street and disappeared
into the park.

Ellie waited at the traffic lights to
cross the road safely, then she headed
to the old oak tree where she'd first
met Shazza. She saw the bird strutting
around on the ground, her bright
yellow crest raised angrily.

'What?' Ellie asked, glancing
around warily. They had only just

18

found out about the development. Surely it hadn't started already? Everything looked normal.

'Can't you see?' Shazza squawked, her red-black eyes gleaming. 'I dropped my numnums. Look what happened to it!'

Ellie followed the bird's gaze. There, lying on the grass, was Shazza's numnums – a half-eaten Vegemite sandwich that Blake had given her.

'What's wrong with it? Why don't you pick it up and eat it?'

Shazza cocked her head and glared at Ellie. 'Are you mad? It's covered in ants!'

'So?' Ellie wasn't happy about being pulled away from her search for such a silly reason.

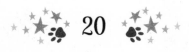 20

'My owner never gave me numnums covered in ants,' Shazza wailed, thrusting her neck out aggressively. 'It's ruined. How can I eat it now?'

'Oh, here you go.' Ellie bent down and brushed the ants off. Then she offered the sandwich to the bird. 'Okay now?'

'Yes.' With a jab of her sharp beak, the cockatoo snatched the food. She grasped it with one clawed foot and tore off large chunks, which she gobbled down quickly. 'Mmm. Numnums.'

Ellie rolled her eyes. She had bigger problems than ants. She looked around the beautiful park. The property developer was going to destroy the park, he was planning to ruin Mum's café, too. Ellie and Blake had overheard him telling his daughter, Felicity, that the new leisure centre would have its own cafés. He said people would rather visit the bright, brand-new complex than the crumbling old café across the road. Then, once Mum's business failed, he would buy their building and redevelop that too!

'There you are, Ellie! I thought you might've come here.'

Blake was running towards her.

He was on his own. He must have left Choccy at home.

'Shazza fetched me because–' Ellie started to say, until she saw what Blake held in his hand. 'Hey! Is that it?'

'Yep! The rest of the article.'

'Well done!' Ellie cried, delighted. 'What does it say?'

'I haven't read it all yet, just the start. I wanted to show you first,' he panted, out of breath. 'But it's definitely the right newspaper. It was still stuck up on the window, that's why we couldn't find it on the floor.'

Ellie grimaced. Why hadn't she thought of that?

 23

'Let's sit down and have a look,' she suggested.

Ellie and Blake sat side-by-side on the bench under the spreading old oak tree. Blake smoothed out the fragile paper carefully and laid it on his lap. Ellie glanced at the remainder of the headline.

'"... lunatic asylum",' she read aloud. Ellie turned pale. 'Isn't that what people used to call mental health hospitals? I know Great-Grandad had a few problems, but this sounds more serious.'

'Where's the other half?' Blake asked. 'Did you leave it behind?'

In reply, Ellie pulled the page out

of her pocket. She laid the two pieces together and read the entire headline. '"Local vet committed to lunatic asylum". Poor man.' She looked at the photo again and was caught by her great-grandfather's intense gaze. 'It looks like he's trying to tell me something.'

'Maybe he was hungry!' Shazza squawked from her perch, gulping the last bite of her sandwich. 'I know how that feels.'

'Quiet, Shazza. This is important.'

'I don't think he wanted to go to the asylum – I mean, hospital,' Blake said, peering at the picture. 'I think "committed" means he was forced to go.'

'Mmm. I agree. What does the article say?' Ellie asked.

'One sec,' Blake clapped his hand on the newspaper as wind gusted through the tree. 'We don't want it to blow away. I'll read it out loud.'

'Go on then.'

Blake cleared his throat. Before he could utter a word, however, a small red squirrel darted down the oak tree. It jumped onto Blake's knee and boldly snatched the newspaper out of his hands.

'Oi!' Blake's shout of surprise turned into one of disbelief as another squirrel ran across the grass from a neighbouring pine tree. 'Wha-?'

The second squirrel grabbed the other piece of paper. This squirrel was larger than the first, and a much more common grey colour. 'Mine!' the grey squirrel said, clutching the paper against its furry chest. 'Hah, my piece is bigger than yours. Loser!'

'No, you're the loser! Mine has pictures!' the red squirrel yelled.

Ellie and Blake watched, open-mouthed, as the squirrels raced back into their separate trees, each grasping a piece of the newspaper article.

Chapter Three

Ellie and Blake gaped at the trees the squirrels had run into. It was hard to believe what they had just seen.

'Hey!' Ellie yelled, springing to her feet. She peered up into the thick branches of the oak tree. 'You bring that back!'

There was no reply.

'Why would they do that?' Ellie asked, baffled.

Blake shrugged. 'Maybe they like to line their nests with paper.'

Ellie gasped. 'They might shred the article! Oi! Come back!'

'There's no point shouting,' Blake said.

'It was like they were competing,' Ellie said, her mind racing. 'Trying to outdo each other with whose piece was best. Are all squirrels like that?'

'Who knows? But, at least you found out what happened to your great-grandfather before they showed up,' Blake said.

 31

'But we didn't read it all! I need to read the whole article!'

'All right. We'd better get it back then.'

'How?'

'Climb, of course. It'll be quicker if we split up. You check out Shazza's tree and I'll go to that one.' He pointed at the tall pine tree that the grey squirrel had returned to.

'Okay ...'

Climb? That was easy for Blake to say! That morning, Blake effortlessly climbed up Shazza's tree when the cockatoo had dropped a drone into the branches. But she wasn't the tree-climbing type. She'd much prefer to sit and sketch under a tree than climb up one!

Ellie watched as Blake started climbing up the pine tree's thick trunk. No way could she do that. She'd probably fall and break an arm.

Ellie looked up at the towering oak tree above her and had an idea. She beckoned to the cockatoo who'd been keeping a beady eye on them.

'Shazza. Can you fly up and find that squirrel's nest?'

'Airrk! Me?' The cockatoo snapped her powerful beak. 'Why should I?'

'Because I fixed your emergency, that's why!' Ellie said, hands on her hips. 'I want you to find that squirrel and get my article back.'

'What if it doesn't want to give it back?'

'Then think of something. Tell it if it doesn't give it back, you'll chomp on its tail or something.'

'But you told me to behave myself and try to fit in with the locals. I don't think that's going to help!'

'Please just do it.' Ellie was running out of patience. 'Or I'll tell Blake not to give you any more numnums.'

Shazza's crest flattened. Without another word, she launched herself into the air and disappeared among the branches.

Ellie waited below. She couldn't see Shazza through the thick cover of leaves, but she heard rustling noises as the big bird fluttered through the branches. After a few moments, she could hear Shazza talking and someone replying, but she couldn't make out what they were saying.

Before long, the cockatoo flew back down and perched on Ellie's shoulder. She didn't have the piece of paper.

'Ouch, watch your claws, they're sharp!' Ellie yelped. 'Didn't you find the squirrel?'

'I did.' Shazza fluttered to the bench and perched on the back.

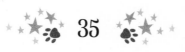

'He wants to have a word with you. He's not very happy.'

'Why?' Ellie asked, arms folded across her chest. 'Because the other squirrel got a bigger piece than him?'

'Exactly,' Shazza said. 'Here he comes.'

The small squirrel edged carefully down the tree trunk and onto one of the lower branches. He had bright red fur, similar to the colour of a fox. His ears were small with long tufts on them, and his tail was thick and bushy. If it weren't for the sadness on his face - and the fact that he had just stolen from her - Ellie would have thought he was cute.

36

'I heard what your wee bird said.'
The squirrel waved his tail slowly, like
a nervous cat. 'But that paper is mine!
You shall not take it from me.'

'I need it,' Ellie replied. She thought for
a moment. There had to be a solution.
'I know. Give me that one back, and I'll
give you another newspaper. A bigger
one. Lots of big newspapers.'

'That's not the point!' the squirrel
shot back.

Ellie was taken aback by how upset he
sounded. 'Then what *is* the point?'

'I am Robbie the Red, the leader of
my clan,' the squirrel said proudly,
even though he looked like he wanted
to cry. 'This is our home. And we are

being invaded! So we need that paper right now!'

'Invaded? Who by?'

'The Greys.'

'Who are the Greys?' Ellie asked, and then she realised. 'Oh. Do you mean those other squirrels?'

'They are not worthy to be called squirrels,' Robbie said, with a wobble in his voice. 'They are intruders, invaders from another land.'

'But ...'

Robbie raised himself to his

full height. His eyes flashed. 'They have taken our trees. They have taken our food. But they will not take our newspapers!'

Ellie was stunned into silence. The red squirrel felt threatened. No wonder he was being so stubborn. Robbie the Red's nose quivered with emotion as he waited for a reply. It was Shazza who ended up breaking the silence.

'Aiiirk! And you thought *I* was difficult!'

'That's because you are,' Ellie said. She turned back to the squirrel. 'Let me get this straight. You're upset because you think the grey

squirrels are taking over your land.
I mean, your trees.'

'Aye.'

'But there's plenty of room for
everyone,' she said, gesturing around
the vast park. 'There are lots of trees.
Can't you just live, like, near each
other?'

'You don't understand,' Robbie said,
looking at his feet. 'The Greys are
different. They want to wipe us out!
They're bigger than us. They're stronger
than us. They're better at finding food.
And some of them carry disease.'

'What sort of disease?' Ellie asked,
wrinkling her nose. 'Do you mean that
they're sick?'

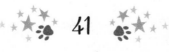

'Ach, you'd think so, but that's not the case. It's called squirrel pox. Greys can carry the disease without getting sick. But if we Reds are so much as exposed to it, we're goners!'

'Well, they can't help that,' Ellie said, trying to sound reasonable. 'I'm sure they're not spreading it on purpose.'

'Well, maybe not. But they're still mean, nasty bullies!' Robbie said. 'Have you met them?'

'I saw the one who snatched the paper-'

'I don't mean just seeing, lass. I said, have you met them? They're a wicked lot.'

Was there really such a thing as a wicked squirrel? Ellie doubted it. She didn't think any animal could ever be wicked. All they ever did was try to survive. Animals weren't cruel or hateful.

'Just wait 'til you meet them,' Robbie said. 'Then you'll know that I speak the truth.'

'And that moment is now,' Shazza said. 'Look behind you ...'

Chapter Four

Ellie turned around and saw Blake striding towards them. Behind him followed two grey squirrels, scurrying to keep pace. Alarmed, Robbie stomped his hind legs on the branch and thrashed his tail.

'It's okay.' Ellie tried to soothe the agitated red squirrel. 'This is a good chance to talk things through. Maybe

you'll find they're not as bad as you think they are.'

'And maybe you'll see that I'm right! I'll stand my ground,' Robbie said, drawing himself to his full height. 'They'll not take this tree!'

Ellie tried not to roll her eyes. Hopefully a nice calm chat would settle things, and then she could get her newspaper article back.

'I couldn't get the paper,' Blake told Ellie as he approached. 'But they want to have a word.'

'With me?' Ellie asked, staring at the grey squirrels. They were indeed much larger than Robbie. They were still very cute, though. Instead of pointy,

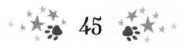

tufted ears like the red squirrel, they had small curved mouse-like ears. Their fur was mostly grey with patches of brown, and their thick, fluffy tails were fringed with silver.

Blake shook his head at Ellie's question. 'No, with you. With the leader of the red group. The grey leader said they might give us back the paper if I brought them here and set up a meeting. They think the Reds might talk if we we're here.'

'Squirrels have meetings?' Things were getting stranger by the minute.

'We'll just be a sec,' Blake said to the squirrels, then he spoke softly, so that only Ellie could hear. 'Um, I've been thinking about your great-grandfather. Well, maybe it's good that the newspaper is gone.'

Ellie took in a sharp breath. 'How can you say that?'

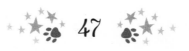

He reached over and patted Ellie awkwardly on the shoulder. 'If your mum thought you should know, she'd have told you by now. And anyway, it might be better to leave them alone.' Blake nodded towards the squirrels who were glaring at each other.

'Yeah, but what if ...' Ellie took a deep breath and explained what was on her mind. 'What if Great-Grandad could talk to animals too? What if that's why he was sent to a mental health hospital? Talking to animals isn't very normal!'

Blake paused. 'You reckon he might have been the one who wrote the numbers on the dial?'

Ellie nodded vigorously. 'It was his house. Who else could have done it?'

'It could have been anyone, really. But your idea makes sense,' Blake went on, speaking a little louder as the squirrels started to sneer at one another. 'Maybe he discovered the magic. Then he wrote the numbers down so he wouldn't forget them.'

'Don't you see what this means?' Ellie said. 'He didn't need to go to a mental health hospital. No more than we do. So we've got to be really careful and not let on what we can do, right? Or else we might also end up like him.' She shuddered.

49

'Yikes, I guess.' Blake pushed the hair off his face. 'All right, let's get that article back then.' He turned to the grey squirrels. 'Okay, guys, have your meeting. Talk to each other.'

Ellie turned to Robbie the Red. 'Give them a chance. They might not be as bad as you think they are.'

Robbie retreated further up the branch as the two grey squirrels ran closer to the tree trunk. 'You think you can get our paper?' the red squirrel boomed at them but still looked a little afraid. 'You cannot have it!'

'Now, don't go getting your tail in a twist,' the smaller and greyer of the grey squirrels said, rising up onto his hind legs. His voice was soft but held a hint of menace. 'You don't wanna get me upset.'

'You don't wanna upset the boss,' the larger grey agreed, running around in tight circles. 'Ain't no one wanna upset Twitching Tony.'

'Settle down, Lumps,' said Twitching Tony, raising a paw. 'We can settle this like reasonable rodents, if we all just stay calm.'

Ellie was amazed to realise that animals had different accents, just like people. She looked at the grey squirrel called Lumps. He had a large swelling on his forehead. Maybe he'd

fallen out of a tree and hurt himself.

'I'll stay calm if you stay calm!'
Robbie said. His fur stood on end,
like a cat when frightened.

'We just want to introduce ourselves properly,' Twitching Tony said. 'I think we got off on the wrong paw before.'

Ellie nodded encouragingly at Robbie. So far, so good.

'And I just wanted to say ... nice tree you've got here.' Twitching Tony came closer and looked up at the stout oak tree trunk. He patted it with a possessive paw. Robbie the Red stood stiffly on his branch and didn't reply.

'It'd be a shame if something were to ... happen to it,' Twitching Tony went on slowly.

'What sort of something?' Ellie couldn't help asking.

'If someone were to ... I don't know ... gnaw the bark off!'

On cue, Lumps exposed his large front teeth. He inched closer to the tree trunk with his mouth open.

'Trees can die so easily,' Twitching Tony said, his voice flat. 'Now wouldn't that be a shame? Then you'd have nowhere to live.'

Chapter Five

'You dare to threaten my home!' Robbie the Red puffed out his fur, trying to make himself look bigger. 'Be gone, and leave us in peace!'

'No need to be like that,' Twitching Tony said. His nose twitched. 'Oh, now look at that,' he said, pointing to his nose. 'You're making me upset.'

'I told you not to upset the boss!'

Lumps cried, rearing up on his hind legs and hopping from foot to foot.

'Down, Lumps. Let me talk to the little red squirrel.' Twitching Tony looked up at Robbie. 'We don't want to destroy your home. We just came here, nice and friendly, to offer you a deal.'

Robbie looked suspicious. 'What sort of a deal?'

'Let's call it insurance.'

Ellie and Blake looked at each other in surprise. 'That squirrel's trying to sell insurance?' Blake asked.

'What's "insolence?"' Shazza squawked. 'Can I eat it?'

Ellie knew a bit about insurance, because her mum had explained it when they moved to their new home.

'Insurance, not insolence,' Ellie corrected Shazza. 'And it's not food. It means you pay someone money regularly. Then, if something goes wrong or breaks, they'll help fix it. Like, if there's a fire or something, the insurance will help pay for the repairs.'

'The human's smart,' Twitching Tony said. 'Like I said, we're offering you a deal. Just ten acorns a week-'

'Wha-?' Robbie blurted.

'And in return,' Twitching Tony went on, 'we'll leave your tree alone.'

This didn't sound like proper insurance to Ellie.

'Do the deal, get the instruments!'
Shazza flew up at Robbie and flapped
her wings. 'Protect my tree!'

Robbie ignored the screeching cockatoo. 'Ten acorns a week?' His voice was shaky. 'I can't afford to pay that!'

'You can't afford *not* to pay it.' Twitching Tony flicked his tail. 'Tell you what, we'll give you some time. Let you think it over.' He turned to his friend. 'Come on, Lumps. Let's go.'

The two grey squirrels turned to leave. Before they went, Lumps stomped hard on a twig. It snapped under his paw. He smirked.

'We'll be back,' Twitching Tony said over his shoulder. 'And then, there'll be no more Mr Nice Squirrel.'

'Yeah. What he said,' Lumps added, kicking up dirt.

The two grey
squirrels swaggered
back to their pine tree,
as if they didn't have
a care in the world.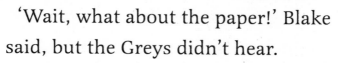

'Wait, what about the paper!' Blake
said, but the Greys didn't hear.

'What nice animals, offering to
look after my tree,' Shazza said. She
preened herself then stared Robbie
in the eye. 'Get the instances!' she
demanded.

'Shazza, it's not really insurance,'
Ellie said, shading her eyes as she
looked up at the cockatoo. 'They're
not trying to help. It's a threat.
If Robbie doesn't pay them what

they ask for, they'll damage the tree.'

'Can they really kill it though?' Blake asked. 'I mean, they're just a bunch of squirrels.'

'Sure they can, lad,' Robbie replied, looking downcast. 'They can strip off the bark, which won't grow back. They can chew through branches and starve the roots.'

'What?' Shazza sounded outraged. 'I'll fly over there right now and bite their fluffy tails!'

'That'll just make things worse,' Blake said. 'We've got to think of a better way.'

'Now do you believe me?' Robbie asked Ellie. 'The Greys are mean.'

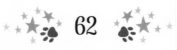

'Yes, sorry,' Ellie said, feeling bad for not believing him. 'You were right. We've got to stop them.'

But Ellie hadn't forgotten their other problem. The whole park was going to be redeveloped to make way for a new leisure centre. If that happened, everything in the park would be destroyed, not just one tree. She didn't want to bring it up, though, because Robbie had enough to worry about.

'There's only one way to stop them,' Robbie said. 'We'll–'

'Hey, you're back! We hoped that we would bump into you again.'

Ellie started at the sound of the voice. It was the two teenage girls that they'd

63

met earlier that day: Ayesha and Sarah.
They were gathering signatures to try to
stop the leisure centre from being built.

'Yeah. Hi.'

'Are you ready to sign now?' Sarah
asked Blake. 'Your friend said you'd

want to.' She held out the clipboard
with the petition.

'Yes.' Blake took it and scribbled
his name on the bottom of the list of
signatures, looking a little sheepish.
When Ayesha and Sarah asked Blake

to sign the petition that morning, he ran away. Blake had thought that having a pool close by may make him feel less homesick for Australian beaches. After talking it through with Ellie, though, Blake agreed the development was wrong.

'Thanks.'

Ayesha was looking up into the branches of the tree. 'Were you ... talking to someone in the tree?' she asked, sounding puzzled. 'There's no one there.'

Ellie glanced up too. Robbie had disappeared. He was probably hiding from the two girls. Shazza was still there, however, preening herself with her beak.

'Were you talking to that bird?'
Ayesha raised an eyebrow.

'No! Of course not!' Ellie forced a
laugh, but it sounded fake even to her.
She didn't want people to think she
and Blake were strange. 'Blake and I
were talking to each other, right?'

Blake nodded. 'Right.'

'But you were looking up there ...'

'We were talking about the bird,
but to each other,' Ellie said, which
wasn't a complete lie.

'Isn't that the bird that snatched our
petition this morning?' Ayesha asked,
gripping the clipboard more tightly.

Sarah glanced at the tree. 'Yeah.
That's the escaped pet your folks are

going to rescue, right?' she said to Blake.

'Err, yeah.'

Ellie knew that wasn't strictly true. Yes, Blake's parents did animal rescues, but he and Ellie were dealing with Shazza themselves.

'Tell them not to leave it too long. Australian birds can't cope with an English winter. Anyway, we'd better get a move on. We still need more signatures.'

Ayesha squinted up at the tree. She didn't say any more, but Ellie could tell she wasn't convinced by what they had said.

'See you guys later,' Sarah said. She linked her arm though Ayesha's and led her away.

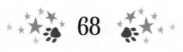

'That was close,' Blake said, wiping his brow. 'We've gotta be more careful.'

Ellie nodded in agreement. She looked back up into the tree and saw that Robbie had reappeared. Maybe if she explained her great-grandfather's story to him, he might agree to give her back the piece of newspaper he had. She opened her mouth to talk, but Robbie spoke first.

'As I was about to say,' Robbie said, 'there's only one way to stop the grey squirrels.'

'How?' Blake asked.

Robbie the Red stood up tall and pointed at the Greys' tree. 'We take the fight to them!'

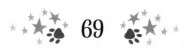

Chapter Six

Ellie didn't like the sound of that. 'What do you mean, take the fight to them?'

'I mean, go over to their tree and see how they like it,' Robbie said.

'You're not going to try to actually fight them, though, are you?' Ellie said, alarmed. 'They're bigger than you!'

'I'm just going to give them a taste of their own medicine.'

Shazza perked up, interested. 'What's medicine? Does it taste nice?'

'Quiet, Shazza. I'm trying to talk to Robbie.' Ellie squinted up at the squirrel. 'Hang on a second. Give us time to think of what to do.'

'Rubbish. The time to strike is now!' Robbie said. He thumped rapidly on the branch with his hind legs. 'Come on, lads!' he called, looking higher up the tree. 'Get yourselves down here.'

As Ellie watched, three red squirrels emerged from the foliage and scurried down the tree. They scampered onto the branch that Robbie and Shazza were perched on, and came to a rest by their leader's side.

71

'This is Wily William,' Robbie
said, waving his paw at the squirrel
closest to him. He was smaller
than Robbie, but his eyes gleamed
with intelligence. 'That's Lorna the

Lionheart, and over there's The Big T. I'd say we're a match for the Greys, aren't we?'

The three new squirrels raised their fists in agreement.

'This is pointless,' Blake said. 'You'll only get yourselves hurt. Like Ellie said, we can figure something else out. We just need time.'

'The time for figuring has passed,' Robbie said firmly. He was no longer upset. He was angry. He turned to Shazza. 'What was it that the Greys were trying to sell us again?'

'Insulation,' Shazza replied, fluttering her feathers.

'Right! We're going straight over there to sell them some insulation!'

'Hang on!' Wily William spoke for the first time. 'What if they *want* us to go over there? What if this whole thing is a trick? Maybe they want us to leave our tree then while we're gone, they'll swoop in and make our wives and kittens homeless.'

'Hmm,' said Robbie and scratched his chin. 'Good point.'

Ellie breathed out a sigh of relief. 'I'm glad–'

'So what I suggest is this, lads,' Wily William interrupted. 'I'll stay here with Lorna the Lionheart and protect the tree. You and The Big T go pay those gruesome Greys a visit.'

The Big T bared his two front teeth. They looked larger and sharper than the other squirrels' teeth, including the Greys'.

'Brilliant,' beamed Robbie.

'They don't call you Wily for nothing. Big T – follow me!'

Wily William and Lorna the Lionheart bounded back up the tree to their families. Robbie the Red and The Big T leapt down the tree trunk quickly and darted across the grass.

'We'd better go too,' Blake said, watching the squirrels run. 'Not you, Shazza,' he said before the bird could join them.

'Aiirk! Why not? I can sell insistence.' The cockatoo raised her crest and jutted her head forward.

'Because you have to protect your tree,' Ellie jumped in quickly, before Shazza could work herself up into

a tantrum. 'You can't
stop the intruders
if you leave,
can you?
The red
squirrels need you.'

Shazza went quiet for a moment.
'That's true.' She snapped her beak
at a sparrow that had fluttered
towards her branch.

'How rude!' the sparrow said,
its feathers ruffled. 'You have the
manners of a goose!' It flew away
again, and Shazza cackled with glee.

'Come on, we're wasting time,' Blake
said, and he took off after the squirrels.
Ellie followed close behind. By the

time they reached the grey squirrels' tree, the trouble had already started.

Robbie the Red and The Big T were standing at the base of the large pine tree. Twitching Tony and Lumps were standing on a branch, along with two other grey squirrels that Ellie hadn't met before.

'Hear that, Nimble Nick?' Twitching Tony was saying. 'They wanna sell us insulation. Now isn't that sweet?'

All four grey squirrels burst out laughing.

Robbie the Red looked confused. 'Why are they laughing at me?' he asked Ellie as she drew close.

'You said insulation, not insurance.

Insulation is what keeps your house warm in winter.'

'Oh ...' Robbie shook himself then started again. 'Like I was saying ... erm ... winter's coming, you know. It'd be a shame ... erm ... if ... if your tree got cold – yes! That's right, don't get cold!'

'You're not very good at this, are you?' Twitching Tony said, the laughter leaving his voice. 'Give it up and pay the acorns. Don't say I didn't warn you.'

Lumps bared his teeth and gnashed them together.

'Never!' Robbie said, finding his voice. 'Come near my bonnie tree again, and we'll fight you tooth and claw.'

'Really?' Twitching Tony hopped down the tree and landed on the grass. He stood face to face with Robbie the Red. 'In that case,' the grey squirrel said, his voice soft and menacing, 'this is war.'

'War it is!' Robbie roared.

'Hold on!' Ellie yelped. Things were moving way too quickly.

The squirrels looked at her.

'How about you call a truce? Just for now. I'm sure we can work something out.'

'Yeah,' Blake added. 'It'll be dark soon. You can't fight at night.'

And we need to get home for dinner, Ellie thought, and we've been out so long that Mum will come looking for us.

'How about we draw a line, halfway between your two trees?' Blake went on. 'No squirrel can cross it until we come back tomorrow.'

'Why would we agree to that?' Twitching Tony said, his nose starting to twitch. 'What's in it for us?'

'Um ... peanuts? You guys like nuts, right? I've got a whole bagful at home.'

'Agreed,' the grey squirrel said. 'As long as we get most of them.'

'No, *we* get the most!' Robbie said.

'Half each,' Blake said firmly. 'And you can't cross the line!'

'My boys will draw the line–' Twitching Tony started to say.

'No deal.' Blake folded his arms across his chest. 'Ellie and I will do it. We don't want any cheating.'

The two squirrel leaders looked at each other. They nodded.

'Great!' Ellie said. 'Now everyone back home, and we will see you tomorrow.'

Chapter Seven

Ellie and Blake spent half an hour gathering sticks. They laid the sticks along the ground halfway between the two trees, creating a boundary line. Thankfully the squirrels kept their word and stayed away. The only problem was Shazza, who kept trying to pick up the sticks and move them. It was only after

another threat to stop giving her numnums that she backed off.

By the time Ellie and Blake got back home, they were tired, grubby and very hungry. What a long day!

'There you are,' Ellie's mum said, as they walked through the café. 'Your parents are looking for you, Blake. You'd better get upstairs.'

'I'm late for dinner,' Blake said. 'I'd better go up. Bye!'

'See you tomorrow,' Ellie said. They nodded at each other. They had agreed to think of solutions to the squirrel problem overnight, then share ideas in the morning.

'Come on, we'd better eat too,'

Ellie's mum said. 'And then get to bed early. Tomorrow's going to be a busy day!'

Ellie agreed, thinking of how hard it was going to be to prevent a squirrel war. But then she realised her mum couldn't possibly be talking about that.

'How come?' she asked.

Her mum looked at her. 'Don't tell me you've forgotten?'

'Of course not. It's ... um ...'

'It's the grand opening! Finally, after all these months, Cattucino will open its doors to the world!' Ellie's mum rubbed her hands together. 'We've already got a

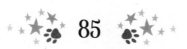

few bookings, but I'm hoping that people passing by will pop in too.'

Ellie nodded, acting as if she'd remembered that all along.

'Everything's got to be perfect,' her mum added. She looked both excited and nervous as she glanced around the café. 'But I keep getting this nagging feeling that I'm missing something. What could it be, though? All the equipment's here, the tables, the chairs ...'

'It all looks great, Mum. Don't worry.'

'Oh, the phone!' her mum chirped. 'That's it. Remember that old Bakelite you found in the storeroom? I wanted to use it as decoration. Now, where did I put it?'

Ellie froze. 'Umm ... maybe you threw it out?'

'I'm sure I didn't. Hang on-' With a jingle of bracelets, her mum swept out of the room.

Ellie shifted from foot to foot. She didn't want anyone else to discover the phone's magic! What if a guest dialled the magic numbers and could suddenly understand what all the cats were saying? What if their secret got out? What if they were all sent away like her great-grandfather? Anything bad could happen!

 87

'I found it!' Ellie's mum bustled back in, carrying the old black phone. 'There,' she said, placing it on a table near the front window. 'How does that look?'

'All right. But are you sure we should have it here?' Ellie asked, thinking

quickly. 'Someone might wreck it. Or
– or one of the cats might jump up and
knock it over.'

'I doubt it,' her mum said breezily.
'Bakelite phones are tough. They
don't make them like this anymore!'

'But it doesn't really fit in,' Ellie tried again. 'Everything else is modern, but this is so old.'

Her mum gave her an odd look. 'What's gotten into you, Ellie? I don't know why you're fussing so much. Anyway, it's dinner time. I haven't had time to cook, so we're having microwave lasagne. Okay?'

Ellie nodded, her mind reeling as she tried to think of how she could convince her mum to remove the phone.

'I'm glad we're opening before you start school.' Ellie's mum continued to chatter as they walked upstairs to their flat. 'I'm going to need your help tomorrow. Just for moral support, if nothing else.'

Ellie smiled weakly. She was meant to be stopping a squirrel war tomorrow and getting the article back! How could she do that, stop people using the magic phone *and* help out in the café all at the same time?

'What time are we opening?' Ellie asked.

'Ten, but we need to be ready before that.'

Ellie and Blake had agreed to go to the park at eight. That didn't give them much time to come up with a plan. Ellie was so anxious that she had trouble sleeping that night.

 91

'Have you thought of anything?' Blake asked the next morning. He was holding the bag of peanuts that he'd promised to give the squirrels if they kept their word.

'Not really,' Ellie said, rubbing her eyes. 'I was thinking about another problem.'

'Like what?'

'The phone. Mum's put it in the café as a decoration. What if someone tries to use it?'

Blake pushed the hair off his face. 'People will come to see the cats, not play with old phones. They probably won't even notice it.'

'But what if they do?'

'Then they'd have to ring the number written on it. Otherwise the magic won't work.'

'Well, *I* rang it.'

'You were bored and on your own,' Blake said. 'Not sitting around in a room full of people and cats.'

'So, you're not worried?' Ellie persisted.

'Yeah, nah. Not much. Let's do one thing at a time,' Blake said. 'First the squirrels, then we'll sort out the phone. I think I know how to fix both.'

'How?' Ellie asked, her spirits rising.

'You'll see.'

As it was still early morning, most of the people in the park were either joggers or dog-walkers. Blake left Choccy at home, and the children rushed straight to the stick boundary to see if it was still there. It was. And so were the squirrels, standing either side of it. They were shaking their paws and threatening each other.

'I said you should come over here and say that!' Robbie the Red was shouting.

Lumps was about to step over the sticks when Blake jogged up with the peanuts. The grey squirrel pulled back to his side of the line.

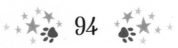 94

'Half each, right?' Blake said. The squirrels cheered and reached for the nuts, but Blake held them out of their reach. 'Wait. First, you've gotta try out my suggestion.'

'We're listening,' Robbie said. 'But make it quick.'

The red and grey squirrels started to bicker again, and Blake held up his hand for silence. 'Ever heard of soccer?'

Ellie stared at him in disbelief. Soccer? Surely he wasn't suggesting a football match between the squirrels?

'It's a game,' Blake said. 'Playing is better than fighting, right?'

'How can a game solve anything?' Robbie asked, his tail waving slowly.

'Sport is good for you. It's healthy competition. Just hear me out.' Blake dug a hand into his pocket and pulled out a plum. He held it down low so that the squirrels could see it. 'This is your ball. Your trees are the goals.

What you do is kick the ball over to the tree, and the other team has to try to stop-'

Blake didn't get to finish his sentence. With a loud screech, Shazza crashed out of the oak tree. She snatched the plum out of Blake's hand and flew up onto a high branch. 'Not a bad snack,' she said, the juices dribbling from her beak. 'I'm still hungry, though. What else have you got?'

Chapter Eight

'Well, that didn't work,' Blake said, watching Shazza trying to crack the plum pit open with her beak.

'Of course not,' Twitching Tony said. 'Why'd we wanna kick things around? Humans do strange things. We need to find food to stay alive, we can't waste time playing games.'

Robbie the Red nodded. For once, he agreed with the grey leader.

Ellie wasn't surprised that the squirrels weren't interested in football. 'Then why waste time fighting? Just talk things through,' she said. She turned to Twitching Tony. 'Tell me, why do you want the Reds' acorns so much? Can't you get your own?'

'How? They've got the only oak tree in the park.' The grey squirrels' nose started to twitch. 'We live in a pine tree.'

'And that's the only pine tree!' Robbie the Red jumped in. 'We love pinecones, but all we get are wee acorns.'

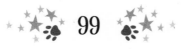

'Maybe we could swap trees with the Greys,' Wily William said to Robbie. 'Then we can have all the pinecones and they can have all the acorns.'

'Ach, no.' Robbie shook his head. 'Sorry, you're not so wily this time. We need acorns *and* pinecones.'

'And so do we,' said Twitching Tony. He glanced at Blake, who was still holding the bag of peanuts. 'And those nuts.'

Ellie and Blake looked at each other. 'Are you thinking what I'm thinking?' Blake asked Ellie. She grinned. 'I think so.'

The children looked at the squirrels and said together, 'Maybe you can do a deal!'

'Whaddya talking about? We already offered the Reds a deal,' said Twitching Tony reproachfully. 'We said we'd sell them insurance, but they said no and–'

'Call that a deal?' Robbie the Red flared up. 'That was nothing less than a threat!'

'Yeah, they don't want insulation!' Shazza squawked. She hurled the plum pit at Lumps. It hit him on the head.

'Oi! Bird! I'm gonna get you for that!' Lumps lunged towards the

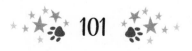 101

tree. Shazza leapt in the air, cackling delightedly.

Twitching Tony watched the cockatoo fly away. He shrugged. 'Threats are how we do business.'

'But you can do it in a better way,' Ellie urged, 'without threats. You can make a fair deal that you're *both* happy with.'

The two squirrel leaders looked at her. Then they looked at each other.

'Ach, I think I see what you're getting at, bonnie lass,' Robbie said, rearing up on his hind legs. 'We can swap wee acorns for pinecones!'

'Exactly!' Ellie looked at Twitching Tony. His nose had stopped twitching.

Ellie thought that was a good sign. 'What do you think?'

'I like it, kid,' he said after a while. 'Robbie the Red, let's talk terms.' He looked up at Blake. 'Then we get the peanuts, right?'

'Right,' said Blake. 'Half each.'

'Before you go,' Ellie said, holding up her hand. 'Can we please have the newspaper pieces back? We can give you other pieces of paper if you like.'

Robbie the Red and Twitching Tony looked at each other and nodded.

'Nimble Nick, go get the newspaper,' Twitching Tony ordered. 'Give it to the nice human here.'

Robbie sent one of his own squirrels

up their tree, then the two leaders walked off, side by side, discussing how many acorns should buy one pinecone.

Ellie waited impatiently for the squirrels to return with the newspaper pieces. Finally, she got them back. They were grubby and crumpled after being used to line nests, but at least they weren't torn further.

'Let's sit down and put them together,' Blake said. They sat on the bench under Shazza's tree. Ellie put the two halves together and smoothed them out. She started reading the article and gasped.

104

'Oh my gosh,' she said, 'look at his name!'

Blake followed her gaze. 'Hmm? Let me see. "Local vet Elliot Granger",' he read out. 'Hey! It say Elliot!'

Ellie was nodding. 'Herriot asked me if my name was Elliot,' she recalled, remembering when she first met the caretaker mouse who lived in the building. At first, Herriot wanted Ellie to move out. He said he was watching over the building, waiting for the return of 'The One' – a man called Elliot. The mice only agreed to let Ellie and the other humans stay in return for an unlimited supply of café crumbs.

'So Elliot was your great-grandfather!' Blake said, his eyebrows raised.

'It makes sense,' Ellie said. 'After he discovered the phone's magic, he must have made friends with the mice.' She paused as she thought it through. 'They must have liked him a lot to be waiting for him after all this time.'

'And he probably used to talk to his patients, too,' Blake said. 'That'd make him a good vet, wouldn't it? Rather than having to figure out what was wrong with the animals, he could simply ask them!'

'That's true. Let me read more.' Ellie was silent as she read the rest of the article. 'It's as we thought. The newspaper says he was unwell because he thought he could speak to animals. And so he was taken away.' Ellie felt tears sting at her eyes. 'How awful! I wish we could have met him. There's so much I want to ask him, like how did he discover what numbers to dial? Now we'll never know. He's dead and it's too late.'

  Blake didn't speak. He took Ellie's hand and squeezed it gently.

Chapter Nine

'We'll have to tell Herriot,' Ellie said after a while. 'Let him know that I'm Elliot's great-granddaughter.'

'And Herriot can probably tell us more about him,' Blake said, excitedly. 'I'm sure there's lots the mice haven't told us. Once they know who you are, they're bound to share!'

'I hope so.' Ellie said, but she couldn't get excited like Blake.

'Why do you look so worried?'

'What will Herriot do when he finds out?' Ellie said, her shoulders hunched. 'All his ancestors were caretakers too. They've been waiting for my great-grandfather for generations. What'll happen when they find out he's never coming back? They might try to kick us out again.'

Blake shrugged. 'She'll be right,' he said, which meant that everything would be okay. 'They'll still want crumbs, so I don't think they'll cause trouble in the café–'

 110

'The café!' Ellie cut Blake off. 'It's opening this morning, and I'm supposed to be helping mum! I hope I'm not too late.'

Blake checked his watch. 'Quarter past ten. We're only a little bit late. Come on, I'll help out too!'

Ellie smiled at her friend gratefully. Despite having only known Blake for a short time, he was proving himself to be a true friend.

They jogged over to the road and stopped at the traffic lights. Ellie could see people walking into the café across the road. The customers were arriving! Mum would be so happy!

'So, I've been thinking about the phone,' Blake said as they waited to cross. 'We can cover up the magic numbers. Put a sticker over them or something. Then no one can ring them up.'

Ellie grinned. It was a simple but brilliant solution! 'Great! I'll write the numbers down first. Just in case the sticker wrecks them.'

As soon as the traffic lights changed, they charged across the road. Ellie was relieved to see that the phone sat untouched on its table near the window. The café was only half full, but even so it was great to see customers there. Some were already

holding steaming cups of coffee and biting into delicious-looking pieces of cake. Others were simply playing with the cats. Beethoven, one of the naughtiest of Ellie's cats, kept pouncing on peoples' feet and darting away, making them giggle.

Ellie's mum was at the counter talking to a man. Even though the man had his back to Ellie, something about him was familiar. But it was the look on her mum's face that really caught Ellie's attention. Her normally smooth brow was furrowed, and her eyes were blazing.

'I'm sorry, I'm not interested.'
Ellie heard her mum say. Ellie
recognised that tone. Her mum
was trying to be polite, but there
was tension underneath.

'Hey, that's the guy,' Blake said, stiffening beside her.

'What guy?' Ellie asked. Then she realised.

It was the man who'd said he was

going to redevelop the park across the road! He was dressed in a tight suit, just as he'd been when Ellie and Blake overheard him talking on the street to his daughter. His back was straight, his hair was slicked to the side, and he sounded very sure of himself.

Ellie noticed a blonde girl about her own age, crouched on the floor patting Chopin, another one of the café cats. 'And that's his kid. Felicity.'

'I'm offering you a good price,' the developer insisted, his voice getting louder. 'If you wait until later, I'll have to lower my offer.'

'No one's looking at the phone,' Blake whispered. 'This might be a

good time to put a sticker on.'

'Can you do it?' Ellie asked. 'Mum needs me.' Ellie walked over and stood firmly beside her mum.

'No deal,' her mum told the developer. 'We've only just opened, and already I've got customers. I'm going to make a success of this place, you'll see.'

The man laughed nastily. 'You really think you can compete with me? Once my leisure centre's opened, all your customers will come to me.'

Something about his manner reminded Ellie of Twitching Tony when he tried to pressure the Reds into buying 'insurance'.

Ellie's mum spoke through gritted teeth. 'Sir, if you'd like to purchase a coffee, please place your order. Otherwise, kindly leave my café.'

'Oh, I'll leave all right,' he said, his voice as oily as his hair. 'But I'll be back. And then my offer will be lower.'

'The answer will still be no.'

'We'll see.' The man looked around the café. 'Felicity? Leave that piece of junk alone. We're going.'

Ellie's head swivelled. Blake was standing in the middle of the café, already watching in shock. Felicity had left

118

Chopin. She was now standing at the table by the window.

Ellie felt her heart thump when she realised what that 'piece of junk' was. It was the old black telephone – and Felicity was playing with the dial.

Sebastian the Fancy Fox

When their classmate *Felicity* visits the cat café and fiddles with the magical old phone, Ellie and Blake panic that their *secret* is under threat. Before they can find out if Felicity can understand animals too, a *new face* shows up at the door.

New to the park, *Sebastian* and his fox friends are causing quite a stir, scaring squirrels and chasing mice. When Felicity's dog *Princess* gets so frightened that she runs away, Ellie and Blake must use their ability to truly understand Sebastian – and bring Princess *home*.

Read on for a sneak peek at
the next book in the series!

Magic Animal Café

Sebastian the Fancy Fox

Stella Tarakson

Illustrated by
Fabiana Attanasio

Sweet
Cherry

Chapter One

'Felicity? Leave that piece of junk alone. We're going.' The man in the tight suit spun on his heel angrily and swept out of the café. The conversation with Ellie's mum had gone wrong. The man was a property developer who wanted to buy the building they were in off Ellie's mum – but Ellie's mum refused to sell to him. It was where they lived; their home and cat café, not his.

'C-coming, Daddy.' Felicity turned away from the old-fashioned black telephone. Her face paled and she ran out after him.

'D-did you see that?' Ellie stammered as she joined her friend Blake across the café.

Cattucino, the cat café, was on the ground floor of the building. Today was the café's grand opening, and it was already shaping up to be a disaster. Not only had Ellie's mum been hassled by the greedy developer in front of customers, the children were afraid that their big secret was about to be discovered.

Blake nodded. 'That girl Felicity was playing with the magic phone!'

'Do you think Felicity might have' – Ellie swallowed – 'dialled the numbers?'

Blake shuddered. 'I couldn't see. Let's hope not.'

Blake and his parents lived one level above Ellie and her mum. Together, Ellie and Blake had found a mysterious old phone in a trunk. When they dialled the numbers written on the phone, they gained the amazing ability to talk to animals! Although it was exciting, they hadn't told anybody else, not even their parents. At first, they just thought it might spoil their fun, but now they had a more pressing reason to keep quiet ...

It could lead to serious trouble. Just like it had for Ellie's great-grandfather. He was a vet named Elliot and he used to live and work in the building. It seemed that he, too, could talk to animals, but he was sent to a mental health hospital because of it. Ellie and Blake didn't want that to happen to them.

Ellie had tried to stop her mum from putting the phone in the café, but Mum really wanted to.

She thought it looked good near the front window. She had no idea what the phone could do.